Grandpappy

by Nancy White Carlstrom
Illustrated by Laurel Molk

Little, Brown and Company
Boston   Toronto   London

FIRST EDITION

Library of Congress Cataloging-in-Publication Data

Carlstrom, Nancy White.
    Grandpappy/by Nancy White Carlstrom;
illustrated by Laurel Molk.
        p.   cm.
    Summary: Nate's visit to Grandpappy's house
in Maine is filled with such everyday adventures
as finding a four-leaf clover, watching a gray heron,
and shopping for supplies.
    ISBN 0-316-12855-4
    [1. Grandfathers — Fiction. 2. Maine — Fiction.]
I. Molk, Laurel, ill. II. Title.
PZ7.C21684Gr   1990
E — dc19   88-38819
                                                 CIP
                                                 AC

10 9 8 7 6 5 4 3 2 *1*

BP

Published simultaneously in Canada by
Little, Brown & Company (Canada) Limited
PRINTED IN THE UNITED STATES OF AMERICA

For Pappy and Beki,
who walk as light
— N.W.C.

For Peter and my family
— L.M.

This is the way my Grandpappy sings
when the day is new
and there's dew on the grass.
He throws his head back
and lifts his voice to the sky.
And I sing too.
It's good to be at Grandpappy's house.

We eat breakfast and take turns
looking through the binoculars.
The gray heron is bending low for his morning meal.
Grandpappy says, "We don't work that hard for our flapjacks a
Do we, Nate?"

This is the way my Grandpappy looks at the ground
when we walk to town.
Like a bird himself. All bent over.

But he finds four-leaf clovers and old keys
and even a ten-dollar bill once.

After we bought supplies that time
(Grandpappy never says "groceries")
we divided up the money.
Grandpappy slipped some of his
into Mattie Mae's old red sweater
while they were talking
outside the store.
He didn't know that I saw.
Grandpappy always says that people
are more important than things.

This is the way my Grandpappy laughs.
It comes up slowly from deep down inside
and spills out and over like the milkshakes
we make in the blender for lunch.
There's no place to hide from Grandpappy's laugh.

This is the way my Grandpappy climbs
over rocks as we head down the beach.
One foot up . . . wait . . . pull a leg . . . stop.
"Come on, boy, get in front of this slow old geezer!"
he says.
But I follow him until we reach the cove where
the seagulls sit.

We fling them stale bread
and then swing our arms in the air.
When our hands touch
we turn and walk together on the wet sand.

This is the way my Grandpappy smiles,
all crinkly around the corners of his eyes,
when he hears me talk.
"You sound just like your daddy, Nate,
when he was a boy. But you're a better stone skipper."

This is the way my Grandpappy thinks
when he sits on a log that the tide brought in.
He squints up his eyes and taps his fingers
on the palm of his hand.
He rubs his beard and looks far out to sea.

"Is it a selkie, Grandpappy?"
He laughs and says, "No. No. I was just thinking.
About the year my buddy tried to walk on water."
"What year was that?
"Nineteen forty-two."

This is the way my Grandpappy sleeps
in a chair by the door before supper.
His floppy hat covers his face.

I shake him awake gently
and he says he's only closing his eyes for a bit.
It makes the chowder cook faster.

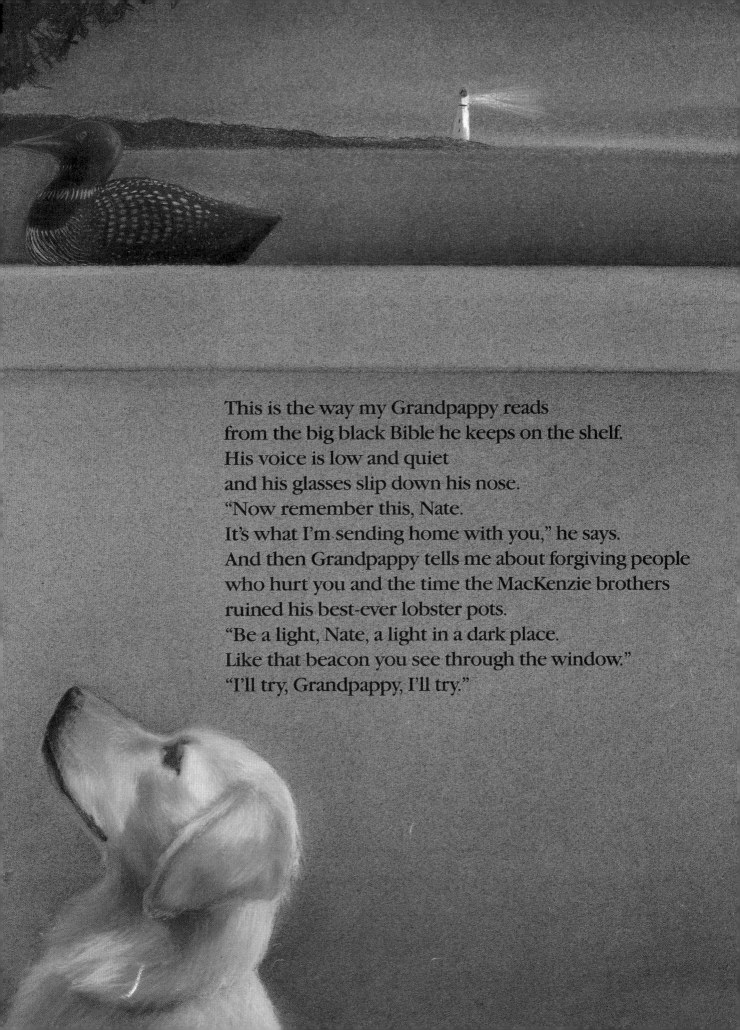

This is the way my Grandpappy reads
from the big black Bible he keeps on the shelf.
His voice is low and quiet
and his glasses slip down his nose.
"Now remember this, Nate.
It's what I'm sending home with you," he says.
And then Grandpappy tells me about forgiving people
who hurt you and the time the MacKenzie brothers
ruined his best-ever lobster pots.
"Be a light, Nate, a light in a dark place.
Like that beacon you see through the window."
"I'll try, Grandpappy, I'll try."

This is the way my Grandpappy walks when his slippers
slide into my room at night.

"Still awake, Nate?" he asks.
Then he takes me out to see the stars.

He puts his hand on my shoulder as we look up.
"It's okay to feel small, you know.
Small, but not alone,
and dressed in glory like the stars."

This is the way my Grandpappy cries
when we say good-bye.
He sneezes and coughs and pretends it's a cold.
But I know he is sad to see me leave.
We hug and kiss.

Grandpappy doesn't say he will miss me.
But I know he will.
Instead he says, "Go on now. Climb up onto
that old iron horse and don't look back."

But I always look back. And so does he.
This is the way it is with Grandpappy and me.